ROB CHILDS

THE BIG STAR

Illustrated by Aidan Potts

YOUNG CORGI BOOKS

THE BIG STAR
A YOUNG CORGI BOOK : 0 552 52825 0

First publication in Great Britain

PRINTING HISTORY
Young Corgi edition published 1995
Young Corgi edition reprinted 1995, 1996

Set in 14/18pt New Century Schoolbook by
Phoenix Typesetting, Ilkley, West Yorkshire.

Young Corgi Books are published by Transworld Publishers Ltd,
61–63 Uxbridge Road, Ealing, London W5 5SA,
in Australia by Transworld Publishers (Australia) Pty Ltd,
15–25 Helles Avenue, Moorebank, NSW 2170,
and in New Zealand by Transworld Publishers (NZ) Ltd,
3 William Pickering Drive, Albany, Auckland.

Printed and bound in Great Britain by
Cox & Wyman Ltd, Reading, Berkshire.

Pud was boiling inside, but when he spoke, his words were icy-cold. 'I'd rather be like I am than trying to act like somebody else,' he hissed. 'You're just a sad copycat of your uncle!'

Nobody had ever stood up to Carl like that before and he didn't know how to react. He glared at Pud in simmering silence for what seemed like an age, but the burly Danebridge number nine never flinched.

'C'mon, then, *superstar*,' Pud taunted him. 'What are you waiting for? Having to work out what Dizzy Dazzler would do first, are you?'

ROB CHILDS is a Leicestershire teacher with many years experience of coaching and organizing school and area representative sports teams. This is his ninth book about the Weston brothers to be published by Young Corgi Books.

Dedicated to my Grandad, with
many happy memories

1 Opportunity Knocks

'What a goal!'

The scorer's boast was loud enough for everyone to hear. 'That's my second,'he cried. 'The keeper never stood a chance.'

The goalkeeper, reluctantly, was forced to agree. Chris Weston looked around at what was supposed to be his defence. It was a shambles. 'Where was the marking?' he complained. 'Who's supposed to be picking up that big number nine?'

'Er, I guess I am,' said Philip sheepishly. The lanky centre-half was sitting on the penalty spot, staring in disgust at his long legs stretched out uselessly in front of him. 'Fell over my own clumsy feet going for the ball – sorry!'

Chris sighed. Philip Smith was his friend and teammate at Danebridge Primary School and both of them had been hoping to catch the manager's eye today. It was a trial for the Area soccer squad.

'Don't worry about it, Phil,' Chris said. 'Can't be helped. Just try and stick as close as you can to that kid. He's getting too much room.'

'He needs it for his head,' Philip

8

grunted, hauling himself slowly up.

Chris sniggered and booted the ball back upfield where he could see the scorer still exchanging hand-slaps of congratulations. 'Yeah, I know what you mean. He's starting to get on my nerves, too. Who is he?'

'Dunno, Carl somebody, I think. But it's my bad luck to be playing against him today, I know that,' said the defender.

Chris nodded in sympathy. 'He's good all right, I have to admit.'

'Trouble is, he knows it,' Philip answered, 'and makes sure everybody else knows it, too.'

'C'mon, cheer up!' Chris smiled. 'We've still got time to show him what *we* can do. We don't want to let him have another.'

Less than a minute later, though, the same striker was on target once more. He was almost as tall as Philip, but more athletic in build, and his power made him a threat in the air as well as on the ground. He timed his jump for a cross better than his marker and headed the ball firmly towards the top corner of the net.

'Goal!' he screamed – but it wasn't.

Chris had taken off as if he'd used a trampoline and, at the last second, finger-tipped the ball just over the bar.

'Hey! Wicked save, man!' cried the attacker, running his hands through his close-cropped black curls in disbelief. 'Dead cert goal, that.'

All the people watching had thought so, too. It was the first opportunity Chris had really had to shine and make his mark on the game. On the touchline, Mr Taylor, the Area team manager, put a little tick in his notebook against the name of Chris Weston.

There were a growing number of ticks down his list of players who had been sent along by their schools to the Area trial. Mr Taylor also liked to add star symbols to some of these to remind him of the ones who had especially impressed him with their skills.

The biggest star so far was drawn alongside the lad wearing the number nine yellow training bib, Carl Diamond.

Carl introduced himself as he yanked Chris back up onto his feet. 'Great stuff there, man. Not many keepers can stop my efforts going in.'

'Thanks,' Chris said modestly, returning his grin. 'Can't go letting you score every time.'

'2-1 to me, I make it, and there's plenty more to come.'

'More saves or more goals?' asked Chris cheekily.

'More goals for me, man, of course,' Carl bragged. 'You'll need a calculator to keep count.'

Philip managed to head the corner out of danger and Carl sauntered away, in no hurry to leave as the defenders moved up towards the halfway line. It wasn't a very well organized offside trap. The boys were playing together for the first time and hardly even knew each other's names yet. As the Yellows regained the ball, a full back in a blue bib was still lingering too deep in his own half, keeping the attacker onside.

Carl pounced onto a quick pass like a panther and loped clear for goal. The full back was too far away to challenge him, and no other defender could get back in time. It was one against one, goalscorer versus goalkeeper.

Chris raced out of his goal to try and narrow the shooting angle and to

dive for the ball at the forward's feet, if necessary. He never even got close. As soon as Carl saw him coming, he hit his shot in full stride.

The ball soared over Chris's head and he hoped for a moment that it was going over the bar. Then a groan of dismay escaped from his throat as he turned to watch it swing and dip down to smack into the net.

'Goal number three!' Carl whooped. 'A hat-trick!'

He sprinted off towards the touch-line and performed a well-rehearsed, tumbling routine right in front of Mr Taylor. It started with a cartwheel, then a handspring and Carl finished it all off with a high forward somer-sault to land perfectly on his feet. He stood straight and proud, arms raised to the sky in salute, as if waiting for the others to run up and worship him as their hero.

'Huh! What a show-off!' Philip muttered. 'He must think the TV cameras are here.'

Even Mr Taylor thought the boy was overdoing the celebrations somewhat. 'OK, Carl, thank you,' he called out. 'Good goal, but we can do without all the gymnastics. This isn't the Cup Final, you know. Take a break now for a bit, so we can try somebody else out in your position.'

Carl scowled and tore off the yellow bib, tossing it at another boy. It landed on the ground at his feet and Carl stomped away towards a group of cheering pals from his own school, Highgate Juniors.

The Area manager was not

amused. 'A bit too big for his boots, by the look of it,' he remarked, putting a question mark against the star in his book. 'Pity!'

'Well, I did warn you about his attitude,' said the Highgate teacher nearby. 'Takes after his uncle, I gather. Diamond's rated the best footballer in Africa, but Carl wants to be the best player in the world some day.'

'Acts like he is already!' Mr Taylor grimaced. 'Or at least the best acrobat in the world!'

2 Secret Weapons

Mr Taylor swapped players on and off the pitch throughout the Area trial to give all of them a fair chance to show their talents.

Some lads, like Philip, felt a little too nervous to be at their best, but Chris managed to produce glimpses of his true form, despite Carl's goals. Among the goalkeepers on view, he handled the ball as well as anyone and pulled off a number of saves. The Danebridge captain was thrilled at the end of the session to be chosen for a second trial, but Philip's name wasn't called out.

'Well done, everyone,' Mr Taylor told them. 'I'm only sorry we can't invite you all back again. Perhaps I'll be able to see you play for your school instead another time.'

'Hard luck, Phil,' said Chris, 'but you heard what he said.'

'Nah!' Philip replied. 'He was just saying that to make us feel a bit better. That Carl wrecked my chances today. He made me look a fool.'

'No he didn't. You played OK against him when he came back on later.'

Philip chuckled. 'Only 'cos he

started sulking after Mr Taylor told him off for moaning at other kids' mistakes. He wasn't really trying.'

'Just hope I'm on his side, anyway, next week,' Chris smiled, 'and then maybe I won't let so many in.'

Chris's grandad had been watching and had his own views about Carl Diamond. 'He's a talented lad, no doubt about that, but he's still got a lot to learn.'

'How's that?' asked Chris. 'He's dead good.'

'Dead lazy as well from what I saw of him,' Grandad replied as the boys clambered into his car for the ride back to Danebridge. 'He didn't seem to want to play for the team at all, just for himself.'

'That's right,' agreed Philip. 'If the ball wasn't passed straight to him, he didn't usually bother to chase after it. He just gave up.'

'Anyway, forget about Carl,' Chris said. 'We've got Great Norton at home in the League on Saturday. Should be a good game. They had four lads there at the trial.'

'Yeah, Dan, their captain, said they won their first match, just like us.'

'But they haven't seen Danebridge's secret weapons yet, have they?' Chris giggled. 'They're in for a shock!'

'Pud and Jamie, you mean?' Philip smirked. 'Even we don't know half the time what those two are going to do next, so the opposition's got no chance!'

Great Norton soon felt the full force of David Bakewell – 'Pud' to his pals, so long as they knew he was in a good mood.

When a player the size of Pud started to throw his weight about on the football field, someone else was sure to come off the worse for wear. This time it was Wayne, their goal-keeper, who was flattened by the human steamroller when Pud challenged late for the ball. Wayne thought he already had it safely in his arms but Pud proved him wrong. The bulky attacker made no attempt to veer out of the way but ploughed straight on, knocking both the keeper and the ball into the back of the net.

Mr Jones, the referee and head-

master of Danebridge School, immediately blew his whistle. 'No goal! That was a deliberate foul, David. Cut out the rough stuff, do you hear me?'

Pud nodded, but it didn't stop him gloating. He had no sympathy for goalkeepers, not even for Chris, his own captain. Pud always belted the ball as hard as possible, and if any keeper got in its way, he reckoned it was their own stupid fault. A jagged hole in the wooden planking of the changing hut was ample proof of the power of his shooting.

While Wayne was still a little groggy from the collision, he was called into action again. This time he stopped one of Pud's special master-blasters from close range and quickly wished he hadn't. It bent his fingers back painfully and he wisely decided he'd had enough for one match.

After what had happened, nobody else was exactly keen to take his place between the posts, and the brave vol-unteer's nervousness soon cost the visitors a goal.

Little Jamie Robertson, the youngest player on either side, was

up to his usual tricks down the Danebridge left wing. He loved to skip along the touchline with the ball under close control, baffling opponents with his dribbling skills. Often he overdid it and lost the ball, but this time his speed left three defenders sprawling in his wake. He fooled another with a rapid double-shuffle of his dancing feet and then fired at goal.

The substitute goalie appeared to have the shot covered at the near post until Pud arrived. The boy heard Pud's heavy, thudding approach, and fatally took his eye off the ball. In that vital split-second, he let it slip in between his legs and over the line.

'Lucky!' growled Pud as he lumbered over to ruffle Jamie's ginger hair.

'What do you mean?' Jamie protested. 'All my own work, that goal.'

'Rubbish!' Pud scoffed. 'It was me who put that kid off. Scared of me, he was.'

'Not surprised, seeing two tons of blubber heading his way,' Jamie answered back cheekily, scuttling out of Pud's reach.

Pud waved his fist but knew there was no point in trying to catch him. Jamie was too fast. 'I'll fix him later for that,' he promised himself under his breath.

Try as they might, Danebridge could not build on their lead by half-time, and early in the second period, Great Norton broke away to score a fine goal themselves to equalize. After Pud rattled the crossbar, Dan Robson collected the rebound and started a quick-passing move up the right wing. He finished it, too, running the length of the pitch to turn a low centre expertly past Chris into the Danebridge net.

There was no further scoring and both teams had to be satisfied with a 1-1 draw and one point apiece. The two captains shook hands after the final whistle. 'Thought we had you beat there today,' said Chris.

'This team of mine never gives up,' Dan grinned and then added, 'but I wish we had a couple of attackers like that little left winger of yours and the

fat kid. Why didn't they go along to the trial?'

Chris smiled, wondering what Pud would have done if he'd heard how Dan had described him. 'Perhaps because they both tend to lose things too easily. One loses the ball, and the other loses his temper!'

Dan laughed. 'Maybe so, but I bet you won't lose many matches this season with the pair of them in your team.'

3 Trial and Error

'C'mon, man, quick. Give me the ball.'

Carl Diamond's loud demand made his teammate panic, thinking there was an opponent right behind him. His hurried kick went over Carl's head and the new Selworth Area team captain made no attempt to run after it.

'What kind of a pass d'you call that, man?' Carl snarled. 'You're useless.'

Mr Taylor, supervising the trial match, shook his head. He was already having second thoughts about his decision to make Carl captain. 'Too late now to change my mind,' he told himself. 'Have to give the boy a chance to show he *can* become a good leader.'

The manager was hoping the extra responsibility of being captain would make Carl try harder to help the other players. He knew they needed his goal-scoring ability, but not at the expense of poor team spirit.

A typical example of Carl's very special skill was soon provided. And what a stunning goal it was! Dan Robson began the move by playing a neat one-two with the winger, and then curling an accurate centre into

the goalmouth. Carl met it with a dramatic scissors-kick about a metre off the ground and the ball thwacked into the netting behind Chris before he'd barely had time to blink.

The keeper had expected Carl to control the ball first, and the high-flying volley had taken him completely by surprise. As Carl went roaring off to do his acrobatics again along the touchline, Chris heard an all-too-familiar, slightly mocking voice.

'Magic goal, eh? You never even saw it.' It was Andrew, his elder brother, leaning casually on the goalpost.

'What are *you* doing here?' Chris sighed.

'You don't sound very pleased to see me.'

'I'm not.'

'Oh, thanks. Just when I came along especially to see you as well.'

'Only so you could laugh when I let a goal in.'

Andrew smirked. 'Would I do a thing like that, little brother?'

Chris rolled his eyes. 'Thought you'd got a soccer practice yourself at school.'

'Yeah, played a blinder as usual. And now I've come over here to support you.'

'Come to cadge a lift home with Grandad, more like,' laughed Chris. 'But I did cheer *you* on, remember, when you were in the Area team.'

"S'right. That was only a couple of seasons ago. Mr Taylor gave me a little nod when I arrived.'

'That's the end of my chances, then, if he realizes you're my brother,' Chris grinned. 'Selworth always lost when you played.'

'Rubbish!' snorted Andrew. 'That's not true.'

'Seemed like it. What about that superb own goal you scored once . . .?'

'OK, OK, don't remind me, we all make mistakes.'

'Apart from Carl there. If you listen to him, you'd think he was perfect.'

'Is he the kid whose uncle is that African player, Dazzler Diamond?' Andrew whistled. 'Wow! Dazzler scored a fantastic goal in the World Cup. Goal of the tournament, it was.'

'Yeah, yeah, I know. Carl's told us

all about it – only *he* calls it "Goal of the century!" ' Chris muttered, turning his attention back on to the game. 'Now shut up for a bit, will you, I need to concentrate.'

It was just as well that he did. When a long-range shot from Dan swerved its way towards him, Chris managed to get his body right behind his hands. Although the ball spun out of his grasp, it hit his chest and plopped safely back into his grateful arms.

Chris was relieved later, too, to find himself in the squad for the first Area match against City Boys. It was only as a sub, since Wayne from Great Norton had been named in goal, but

Mr Taylor promised Chris he'd play part of the game. 'Nice to see Andy and your grandad again,' he smiled. 'Seems just like old times to have the Weston family back on the scene.'

Sadly, by the time Chris was getting himself ready to come on for the second half, Selworth were already losing 4-1. They had been totally outplayed by City Boys before half-time, and nothing was going right.

Wayne was having a nightmare, at fault with three of the goals. 'My hand still hurts from that school game,' he moaned to Chris. 'Then I got another knock on it near the start today and that's why I kept dropping the ball.'

Carl wasn't willing to listen to any excuses. He was furious. At Wayne, at the defence, at anyone he felt hadn't given him the ball when they

should have done. Apart from scoring their single goal, almost his only other touches were to kick off each time they let another one in themselves.

Mr Taylor was as fed up with hearing Carl's complaints as were the players, and told him to be quiet. The captain slumped down onto the grass in a sulk, paying no attention to the team changes and new tactics that the manager was organizing during the break.

Ten minutes later, Mr Taylor's patience with Carl ran out. The boy seemed to have lost interest in the game and had hardly bothered to leave the centre-circle since the restart. The manager signalled to the referee that he'd like to make another substitution. When Carl gazed idly round to see who was being taken off, he was shocked to see that it was him.

He simply could not believe it. The manager was waving at him to come off the pitch. Carl looked round in horror, still thinking it must be somebody else behind him. He was actually being subbed! It had never happened to him before and he'd never even dreamt that it would. It was a huge blow to his pride.

'Take over as captain, please, Dan,' Mr Taylor called out. 'Get the team going – encourage them.'

As play went on without him, Carl marched up to Mr Taylor. 'Why have you pulled *me* off, man?' he demanded rudely. He was so angry, he forgot that he was talking to a teacher. 'Don't you know who my uncle is?'

'What's *he* got to do with it?' snapped Mr Taylor. 'Your uncle's not in this team – and neither are you at the moment. Just because your name's Diamond doesn't mean to say you can't be subbed, you know.'

'But I'm your captain, man!'

'Don't call me *man*!' Mr Taylor stormed, finding it difficult to control his temper. 'Dan's captain from now on. After your behaviour in this match, you don't deserve that honour any longer.'

Carl staggered backwards. 'Why?' he cried, almost in tears.

'Because I don't think you're the kind of captain the other lads can respect,' Mr Taylor answered. 'At least they know that Dan won't blame them if they make a mistake when they're trying to do their best.'

Carl stood defiantly in front of the manager for several seconds, and then turned on his heel and stalked off back to the changing room.

Mr Taylor sighed heavily. 'Well, if he throws another tantrum like that, he'll be lucky to play at all in the future, no matter how good he is – or even who his uncle is!'

4 Win, Lose and Draw

'Well saved, Chris,' Dan cried out. 'Keep it up.'

Chris had rarely known such a heavy bombardment on his goal. City Boys were a fast, skilful side, the best attacking team he could ever remember playing against. He'd been given no time to himself from the moment the second half kicked off.

At first, with Carl strolling around in the middle of the pitch, it was like playing with only ten men. But as soon as he was replaced, Selworth worked hard together to try and prevent a cricket score.

Chris's own confidence was boosted by a spectacular diving stop in the opening attack, and he was kept so busy that he hit top form. He rose to the challenge of playing at the higher standard of Area football and felt almost as if he could do nothing wrong.

'C'mon,' he urged under his breath as each wave of gold shirts launched itself at the blue Selworth defence. 'I'm ready for you.'

The way the ball was sticking tight in his gloves every time, he began to believe he might even keep a clean sheet. But it was not to be. Just a few minutes before the end, City Boys at last squeezed the ball past him after a corner. Such was their relief, however, that they relaxed their guard and Dan was able to side-foot home a late consolation goal. The final scoreline of 5-2 was not as bad as looked likely at half-time.

'Ah, well!' Chris sighed as he walked off the pitch with Dan. 'I guess at least we can say we drew the second half 1-1.'

'Well played, Chris Weston,' Mr Taylor greeted him. 'Might have been double figures without you. You're the first winner of my "Man of the Match" award.'

'But I only played half the game,' Chris grinned.

'Reckon you deserve a full one next time, then, don't you?' the manager

laughed before turning to speak to Dan. 'And I wish I'd chosen you as captain in the first place. The job's yours now for the rest of the season.'

'Thanks, Mr Taylor, that's great!' Dan beamed. 'I'm sure we'll do better in our other matches. Will Carl still be playing?'

Mr Taylor scratched his chin. 'That's really up to him. I'll have to talk to him again and see how he responds to what's happened today.'

'You could come to watch Carl play next week at Danebridge, if you like,' Chris suggested. 'We've got a league match against his Highgate team.'

Chris broke that piece of news to Grandad, too, on the journey home.

'Carl's bound to be in a bad mood now he's lost the Area captaincy. He'll be out to prove something.'

'*You* certainly did today,' Grandad said. 'That was the best I've ever seen you play. I'm really proud of you.'

Chris blushed at such praise. 'I just want to be a good goalie like you were, Grandad.'

'Well, I like to think you do take after me a bit, m'lad,' Grandad

grinned. 'But you're going to be a far better goalie than I ever was, I know that.'

They exchanged smiles, and Chris was thoughtful for a few minutes. 'Guess Carl has a lot to live up to as well,' he said at last. 'I mean, besides his uncle being a famous footballer, his dad's a doctor in Selworth.'

'Aye, and we all know which one Carl would prefer to be, don't we?' Grandad replied. 'But I reckon it'd be better for him and the team if he'd stop pretending he's old Dazzler all the time. He seems to think he can do what he likes just because of his uncle.'

Chris laughed. 'Yeah, we've all seen

Dazzler on the telly in trouble with referees and doing somersaults and stuff. He does get rather carried away.'

'So does Carl,' Grandad said, and then began to chuckle as a little joke came to mind, the kind of pun that always made Chris groan. 'Maybe he should take a leaf out of his father's book for a change and try to have more *patience*!'

Danebridge Primary School's home game with Highgate Juniors on the village recreation ground was eagerly awaited.

The other players in the Danebridge squad had heard all

about Carl from Chris and Philip. 'Hope we have a chance to see his somersaults,' said Jamie after a lunchtime kickabout on the school's own small playing field.

'I don't,' Philip replied sharply. 'That would mean he'd scored and I got fed up of him doing that at the Area trial.'

Jamie giggled. 'Can you imagine it, if Pud started jumping around all over the place? There'd be an earthquake!'

'Hey, I heard that, Gingernut!' Pud cut in. 'If I wanted to show off like that, I'd make sure I had a soft landing first – right on top of you!'

'You'd be flat enough then to slip inside that sketchbook of yours, Jamie,' Chris laughed. 'Been drawing anything good lately?'

'Better not be any more stupid cartoons of me,' Pud bellowed, juggling a ball up from his foot onto his knee.

'Look who's trying to show off now,' Jamie teased, darting away as Pud lost control.

'Where's his sketchbook?' Pud demanded. 'He's always got it around somewhere. If he's been making fun of me again, I'll kill him.'

'Not of you, Big Fellow, don't worry. I can't fit all of you onto one of my pages,' laughed Jamie, but quickly added, 'Only joking, honest.'

'You'd better be, Carrot-Top,' Pud said with a smirk.

'So what *have* you been drawing?' Chris persisted.

Jamie trotted over to collect the

sketchbook from his bag. 'I've been doing some soccer pictures, look. Here's Philip heading the ball.'

'You've given me a neck like a giraffe,' Philip protested half-heartedly, secretly quite pleased at the result. 'And legs like a grasshopper!'

'Well, they're meant to be funny,' Jamie grinned, flicking over a page. 'This one's of the skipper, making a flying save.'

Chris gazed at the picture of a goal-keeper with wings, taking off and catching the ball in full flight. 'Wish I could sprout wings like that,' he chuckled. 'They'd come in useful sometimes!'

'I'll show you some of Pud later,' Jamie whispered, giggling. 'When it's safe.'

'You could do one of him kicking Carl around like a ball, making him turn somersaults up in the air,' Philip suggested.

'Sshh! Don't go giving Pud any ideas,' Chris grinned. 'We'll deal with Carl our own way. If we want to win this game, we'll have to stop him getting the ball and make him become more and more frustrated.'

'Easier said than done to keep Carl quiet,' Philip muttered.

5 Nobody's Perfect

Carl Diamond stood at the top of the changing hut's small flight of wooden steps, gazing out at Danebridge recky. He posed there in the all-white kit of Highgate Juniors, as if photographers were jostling below to take his picture for the newspapers.

He liked to imagine he was about to stride out on to the famous turf of Wembley Stadium, but the reality in front of him did not quite match his daydream. The village pitch was

large enough, but it had hard, bare patches in some places and long grass in others.

Carl pulled a face and glanced back into the ramshackle hut to see if the rest of his team were ready. 'C'mon, you guys,' he called out, knowing the boys in the 'home' changing room next door would hear too. 'Let's go out and thrash this lot. They can't be much good playing on a crummy ground like this.'

Pud jerked up from tying his laces, right boot resting on the bench. 'Crummy ground!' he choked. 'Who does that kid think he is?'

'The greatest!' Philip sighed, pulling on his red and white striped shirt. 'Or reckons he's going to be when he's older.'

'He's not gonna *get* any older, if he carries on talking like that,' muttered Pud. 'I can see we'll have to bring him down a peg or two.'

'Is he as good as Dazzler?' asked Jamie in a low voice.

'Why are you whispering?' Pud said loudly. 'Carl Diamond doesn't dazzle, he drizzles!'

Carl ignored the taunt. He expected others to be jealous of him. Then he noticed Mr Taylor near the pitch, talking to the referee. 'Right, I'll show *him* a thing or two,' he decided. 'I'll show 'em all that you don't rubbish Carl Diamond. He's different class!'

He kicked a ball high into the sky as he led Highgate out on to the pitch, smashing it towards goal on the volley as it dropped. The Danebridge boys tried to avoid watching him parade his skills as they warmed up, but he was the kind of player who attracted the eye like a magnet.

Carl revelled in all the attention. He flicked a football up to balance it on his forehead, then rolled it over onto his neck and down his spine to back-heel it straight to another player.

Pud scoffed. 'He's nothing but a circus act. Let him try and do any fancy stuff like that in the game and I'll bulldoze him into the ground.'

'You're just jealous 'cos you can't do it,' Jamie teased him.

'Bet you can't either, Freckle-Face.'

'No, but I can do something else. You wait and see.'

For the first ten minutes Carl dominated the match, demanding the ball all the time. He took charge of every

corner, free kick and throw-in that Highgate had. If it had been possible, he would have wanted to take the corner and then race into the middle to head the ball into goal himself!

When other players failed to make the most of the chances he created, however, his impatience began to show through. If an attack broke down or a pass went astray, Carl was quick to accuse somebody else of the mistake. It was never his fault. Soon, he refused to pass the ball at all, shielding it from challenges skilfully with his body until sheer force of numbers would crowd him out and block any shot at goal.

The longer the match went on, the more likely it seemed that Danebridge would score first. And if the goal itself, when it came, was hard enough for Carl to bear, the mocking celebrations afterwards were more than he could stand.

Jamie had been practising back somersaults in the school gym club and also on his garden lawn in football boots ever since he heard about Carl's antics. As soon as he saw his left foot shot skid past the keeper's grasp into the net, Jamie scampered off towards the touchline so that nobody could get in his way. He needed space to perform his party piece.

Jamie's teammates had known nothing about his plans. They burst out laughing as he followed up his acrobatic tumbling sequence with a brief jiggle of his hips in front of the corner flag.

Carl felt insulted by the mickey-taking and gave Jamie the dirtiest of looks before he kicked off. When the ball was elsewhere and he thought no-one was watching, Carl ran right into the little winger, catching him a painful crack on the leg.

'That's for being cheeky,' he snarled. 'Don't ever do that again, man, I'm warning you.'

Jamie may have been small and two years younger than Carl, but he wasn't afraid to stick up for himself with bigger lads. This time he didn't have to. Pud suddenly stepped in between them – but not exactly as a peacemaker.

Pud grabbed the front of Carl's shirt in his fists and yanked the tall striker's face down to his own level. 'Listen, *man*,' he growled, deliberately using Carl's own favourite word.

'I saw what you did. Touch my mate again and you'll have to deal with me.'

'Any time, fat boy!' Carl sneered, pulling away. 'Just try it.'

It was only Jamie hanging on to Pud's arm that prevented a fight from breaking out on the pitch. 'Don't hit him, Pud, he's not worth it. You'll only get yourself sent off.'

Pud was boiling inside, but when he spoke, his words were icy-cold. 'I'd rather be like I am than trying to act like somebody else,' he hissed. 'You're just a sad copycat of your uncle!'

Nobody had ever stood up to Carl like that before and he didn't know how to react. He glared at Pud in simmering silence for what seemed like an age, but the burly Danebridge number nine never flinched.

'C'mon, then, *superstar*,' Pud taunted him. 'What are you waiting for? Having to work out what Dizzy Dazzler would do first, are you?'

The jibe jerked Carl out of his trance. 'Don't talk about my uncle like that, man. I don't need his help. I can look after myself.'

'Prove it!' challenged Pud.

Carl might well have done, too, if he'd been given the chance. But at that very moment Mr Taylor spotted the showdown between the two boys. 'Break it up,' he ordered from the touchline. 'Go and cool off, Carl, and get your mind back on the game. Your team needs you – you're losing.'

All the hot air leaked out of Carl like a punctured balloon. His shoulders slumped and he wandered away by himself into the centre-circle, head down.

'Phew, that was close!' breathed Jamie. 'Good job there wasn't a scrap. You might never have played for Danebridge again!'

'Yeah, but I couldn't just let that

big-mouth bully get away with what he did,' Pud said, grinning now. 'I'm the only one round here allowed to use you as a punch bag!'

The second half of the match turned out to be a disappointment. Neither team were able to create many clear chances and only Carl managed to put his name on the scoresheet as usual. Unfortunately for him and for Highgate, it was their net that Carl found – the first time in his life that he'd suffered the agony of scoring an own goal!

Normally he didn't bother doing any defending, but the threat of Philip's height made him go back to mark the gangling defender at a

Danebridge corner. They rose for Pud's powerful kick together, but Philip's aerial challenge made Carl misjudge his header and the ball glanced off him into the net.

Carl was horrified, staring blankly around him, unable for once to pin the blame on others. Nobody in his side dared say anything, but Carl expected all manner of ridicule from

the Danebridge players. To his surprise and relief, none came. The home team were happy enough with the goal and didn't need to gloat. Even Pud somehow resisted rubbing it in.

Philip had no difficulty in marking a dejected Carl out of the match after that, barely giving him another touch of the ball. Danebridge won 2-0, and the trickiest thing Chris had to do was to keep a straight face when consoling his opposing captain at the end of the game.

'Tough luck, Carl. Nobody's perfect!'

Carl nodded sadly. 'No, guess not, man, not even me. Not all the time, anyway . . .'

6 Man of the Match

'Is that big-head, Carl, playing today?' Andrew asked, slumped in the back seat of Grandad's car next to Philip as they drove to the Area game.

'Dunno, don't think so,' answered Chris from the front. 'Might be one of the subs with Phil and Wayne.'

'It'll be a bit of a come-down for him, if he is,' chipped in Philip, thrilled to be included in the Area squad himself after his recent display against Carl. 'He won't like it.'

Andrew laughed. 'He'll just have to lump it, then, won't he? It's his own fault for boasting the way he does.'

'Huh!' Chris snorted. 'Listen who's talking.'

Grandad spoke up before the brothers could fall out. 'Carl's been a poor sport. He has to learn that nobody is bigger than the team, no matter who he is. He can't take his place for granted.'

'Reckon Selworth will win today, our kid?' Andrew began casually, opening the way for the sting to his question. 'Even with *you* in goal?'

'Ha, ha, very funny!' Chris shot back. 'Don't see why not, especially if Mr Taylor thinks he can afford to leave Carl out the side.'

It was an away game in another part of the county, but Chris's map-reading skills were good enough to

direct Grandad to the right school with only one wrong turning.

'Glad you made it OK,' Mr Taylor greeted them. 'And pleased to see Andy here as well to lend support.'

'Got my boots with me just in case,' Andrew joked.

Mr Taylor laughed. 'Sorry, Andy, you're a bit too old for us now.'

'You could always pretend I'm just big for my age!'

'I've got to use that excuse for Carl and Philip,' the manager smiled. 'Carl's already here – he was the first to arrive.'

'Must be trying to get back into your good books,' Grandad chuckled.

'His apology certainly helped. His

father brought him to make sure he said sorry for the way he's been behaving,' Mr Taylor said. 'Carl knows he's starting as sub, but I've told him he'll probably come on for the second half.'

As soon as the match kicked off, however, the Area manager realized they were in for a tough game. Selworth were pressed back on the defensive and their own attacks were rare. Chris made a number of saves but he enjoyed some good fortune as well, especially when his woodwork was rattled twice within the space of a few minutes.

Astonishingly, when Chris *was*

beaten at last, it was only an equal-
izer. Selworth had already snatched a
shock lead on a breakaway raid, completely against the run of play. With
the score still 1-1, they were grateful
to hear the referee's whistle for the
half-time breather.

'Well battled, lads, but we're lucky
to be on level terms,' Mr Taylor said.
'I'm making a couple of changes to try
and improve things, bringing on
Philip to strengthen the defence and
Carl up front.'

'C'mon, team!' Dan rallied them as
they took the field again. 'They were
all over us first half. Now let's give
them a taste of their own medicine.
Get the ball up to Carl quickly.'

Dan set the right example straight

away. He won the ball with a crisp tackle in midfield and pushed it through to Carl. The pass was a little bit ahead of the striker and Carl might well have given it up previously. Not now. He ran on to it with determination, his speed taking him clear of his marker, and he hammered a shot at goal. The ball flashed just wide of the far post.

'Great effort, Carl!' called Dan. 'That's the way.'

Carl grinned. 'Just give me plenty of the ball, man, and I'll do the rest.'

He was as good as his word. The other players had never seen Carl work so hard before and he even applauded their efforts too. He was causing so much panic in the home defence that mid-way through the half, he won a penalty. He'd turned cleverly with the ball inside the area and was tripped up as he drew his foot back to shoot.

Normally Carl would have grabbed the ball immediately to leave his team in no doubt as to who was going to take the spot-kick. Nobody, in his mind, could take it better than himself.

This time, though, he tossed the ball to a surprised Dan. 'Captain's job,' Carl grinned. 'It's all yours.'

'Not today,' Dan said, throwing the

ball back into his arms. 'You were fouled, you take it.'

Carl was not going to refuse. He placed the ball confidently on the spot, took three measured steps back and waited for the referee's signal.

The goalkeeper crouched on the line, trying to guess which way the kick would go. To his credit, he was right, but he never stood a chance of saving the penalty. Carl struck the ball with great power, sweeping it past the diving keeper's hands into the corner of the net.

The captain slapped Carl's raised hand in celebration, but they knew that plenty of work remained to be done if Selworth were to hang on to their slender lead. Philip was a tower of strength in defence. Anything hurled at them in the air he headed away, and he hardly put a foot wrong

on the ground either. With Chris also in fine form in goal, the home side began to sense it wasn't perhaps to be their day – and so it proved.

Selworth's hard-earned victory was finally assured when Carl chased a ball just outside the penalty area. He reached it first, got it under control, lost it, won it back again, beat off another challenge and then lashed the ball up into the roof of the net to put them 3-1 ahead.

He was about to set off towards the touchline to do his acrobatics when he suddenly checked himself and resisted the temptation to show off. It was enough to score an excellent individual goal. He ran to fetch the ball instead and carried it back to the centre-circle for the game to re-start as soon as possible. He was still hungry for more.

In the end Carl's appetite had to be satisfied with the two goals, and Mr Taylor made a point of praising his performance in front of everyone. 'I'm delighted that we've seen a new Carl today, and he has to be my *"Man* of the Match!"' he announced, stressing the first word.

'Hey, wicked! Thanks, man . . . ager!' Carl grinned, and the others laughed as he corrected himself just

in time to avoid sounding too cocky. It made him feel good to have real team*mates* at last.

'Reckon he just about deserved it,' Andrew admitted as he stood with Chris and Grandad on the edge of the group. 'Better than you winning the award again, anyway, little brother! What do you think, Grandad?'

'Don't ask me, m'lad,' he replied. 'You know I'm not too fond of these fancy, modern titles for people. Football's always been a team game.'

'But Carl *is* our star player,' Chris added.

'You're all stars to me,' Grandad smiled. 'Especially you two!'

THE END

THE BIG CHANCE
ROB CHILDS

'C'mon, up the Reds!'

It's the beginning of the season and Chris Weston, captain of Danebridge School football team, knows that his team needs goalscorers – players to put the ball in the back of the net.

Two younger boys show promise – nimble Jamie, who can dribble round any opponent, and moody, overweight David (known as Pud), whose cannonball shots are unstoppable. But can Jamie learn to play as part of a team? And can Pud manage to control his temper? When both boys are picked to play for the team in a vital match – the first round of the county cup competition – Chris knows it is up to him, as captain, to help both boys make the most of their big chance . . .

0 552 52824 2

A SELECTED LIST OF FOOTBALLING TITLES AVAILABLE FROM YOUNG CORGI BOOKS

THE PRICES SHOWN BELOW WERE CORRECT AT THE TIME OF GOING TO PRESS. HOWEVER TRANSWORLD PUBLISHERS RESERVE THE RIGHT TO SHOW NEW RETAIL PRICES ON COVERS WHICH MAY DIFFER FROM THOSE PREVIOUSLY ADVERTISED IN THE TEXT OR ELSEWHERE.

☐	0 552 52824 2	**THE BIG CHANCE**	*Rob Childs*	£2.99
☐	0 552 52581 2	**THE BIG DAY**	*Rob Childs*	£2.50
☐	0 552 52662 2	**THE BIG HIT**	*Rob Childs*	£2.50
☐	0 552 52663 0	**THE BIG KICK**	*Rob Childs*	£2.50
☐	0 552 52451 4	**THE BIG MATCH**	*Rob Childs*	£2.50
☐	0 552 52760 2	**THE BIG GOAL**	*Rob Childs*	£2.50
☐	0 552 52804 8	**THE BIG GAME**	*Rob Childs*	£2.50
☐	0 552 52823 4	**THE BIG PRIZE**	*Rob Childs*	£2.50

PUBLISHED BY YEARLING BOOKS,
FOR OLDER READERS

☐	0 440 86318 X	**SOCCER AT SANDFORD**	*Rob Childs*	£2.99
☐	0 440 86320 1	**SANDFORD ON TOUR**	*Rob Childs*	£2.99
☐	0 440 86326 0	**HERE WE GO!**	*Diane Redmond*	£2.99